For Mum,
who taught us to be whole of heart.

The Two-Hearted Numbat

AMBELIN & EZEKIEL KWAYMULLINA

FREMANTLE PRESS
fine independent publishing

There was once a numbat who had two hearts.

Numbat's first heart was a feather, and when he wore it he felt soft and gentle. But Numbat of the Feather Heart was so kind that he spent all his time looking after the other numbats and doing for them things that they should have been doing for themselves, like finding food. Everyone liked Numbat of the Feather Heart — and no one ever noticed how he tired himself out helping others, until he had nothing left for himself.

Numbat's second heart was a stone, and when he wore it he felt powerful and strong. But Numbat of the Stone Heart was so tough that he refused to have anyone help him. No one liked Numbat of the Stone Heart – and no one ever noticed how he worked tirelessly, using his strength to bring new hollow logs to the burrows all on his own.

Numbat found it very troublesome to have two hearts. He decided it would be better to have only one. But Numbat didn't know which heart to choose, so he went to see the oldest and wisest of numbats to ask for her advice.

Eldest Numbat flicked her ears, twitched her whiskers, and said, 'This is a very difficult problem. I must go to my Thinking Log and consider it. Come and see me tomorrow in the Deep Bush, and I will tell you which heart is your true one.'

The next day, Numbat set forth into the Deep Bush.
He hadn't gone very far when a dingo leapt onto the
path ahead of him, snapping and snarling.

Numbat was wearing his stone heart, and he felt brave and strong — much stronger than a dingo. He charged forwards but the dingo knocked him backwards with his paw. Again and again Numbat tried to get past, and again and again Dingo threw him to the ground.

Numbat remembered how everyone liked him when he wore his feather heart. 'Perhaps Dingo will like me too,' he thought, and so he took off his heart of stone and put on his heart of feather. Numbat looked at Dingo with all the gentleness of his feather heart — and the moment he did, he saw that there was a thorny vine of shiny red berries tangled around Dingo's tail.

'Poor Dingo!' said Numbat. 'I see what you were trying to tell me now. You want someone to take the vine away.' Dingo whined unhappily, and Numbat darted forward, using his claws to pull the thorny vine from Dingo's tail.

Dingo gave Numbat a big lick, and bounded off. Numbat scurried on.

Numbat came to a river. His feather heart fluttered in fear. 'It is such a big river, and I am just a little numbat. What shall I do?'

Numbat noticed a magpie perched on a rock, admiring his reflection in the water. He remembered that magpies liked shiny, colourful things, so he showed Magpie the vine that had been tangled around Dingo's tail.

'Look, Magpie!' he said. 'See how shiny and red these berries are? If you fly me across the river, I will give them to you.'

Magpie stared at the berries, and hopped from one leg to the other in excitement. 'Tell you what, friend Numbat,' said Magpie. 'Give them to me now and then I'll take you across.'

So Numbat held out the berries — but the moment Magpie had them in his mouth, he flew away laughing, 'Ha ha! Tricked you, Numbat!'

Numbat was very sad. Now he had no way of getting across the river. He felt so bad that he took off his heart of feather, and put on his heart of stone.

All of a sudden, the river didn't look so terrible after all. 'It's only a little river, and I am a big numbat!' thought Numbat.

Numbat gathered all his strength and in one mighty bound, he leapt across the water.

Feeling very proud of himself, Numbat scurried on until at last he reached the Thinking Log.

'Hey, Eldest Numbat!' he called. 'I'm here! Come out, and tell me which is my true heart.'

Eldest Numbat stuck her head out of the log. 'I don't need to tell you. You already know. Which heart did you use to get here, the feather or the stone?'

Numbat was confused. 'But I used the feather *and* the stone!'

'Silly young Numbat!' said Eldest Numbat. 'Don't you see? Without your heart of feather, you would never have seen that Dingo was not an enemy, but a friend who needed help. And without your heart of stone, you would never have known that you were strong enough to cross the river all by yourself. The true heart that you must choose is both of them.'

Numbat looked at his hearts. Then, for the first time, he put on his heart of feather *and* his heart of stone. The two hearts melted together to make one — a heart that was as strong as stone, and as gentle as a feather. Numbat had his true heart at last.

Numbat grew to be a great leader, and the young numbats would gather around to seek his guidance. Numbat would always say to them, 'I once thought I had to choose between being as strong as a stone, or as gentle as a feather. But now I know that no one is truly strong who does not also have the softness to care for others. And no one is truly caring of others who does not also have the strength to care for themselves.'

Ambelin and Ezekiel Kwaymullina are from the Bailgu and Nyamal peoples of the Pilbara region of Western Australia.

First published 2008 by
FREMANTLE PRESS
25 Quarry Street, Fremantle
(PO Box 158, North Fremantle 6159)
Western Australia.
www.fremantlepress.com.au

Designer Tracey Gibbs
Printed by Everbest Printing Company, China.

National Library of Australia
Cataloguing-in-publication data
    Kwaymullina, Ambelin.
    The two-hearted numbat / Ambelin Kwaymullina and Ezekiel Kwaymullina.
    ISBN: 9781921361234 (hbk.)
    For children.
    Numbat--Juvenile fiction.
    Other Authors/Contributors: Kwaymullina, Ezekiel.
    A823.4

Department of Culture and the Arts
Government of Western Australia

lotterywest
supported